Doctor St. Nick

Jeanie Smith Cash

ISBN:1496091450
ISBN-13:9781496091451

DEDICATION

To Jesus my Lord and Savior, who made this all possible. To my own special hero, Andy. You are always there for me, and I love you so very much. To my sweet family for their love and support. As for God His way is perfect; the word of the Lord is flawless. He is a shield for all who take refuge in Him. Psalms 18:20 .

For you know the plans I have for you, declares
the Lord, plans to prosper you and not to harm
you., plans to give you hope and a future
Jeremiah 29:11

CONTENTS

ACKNOWLEDGMENTS

I'd like to dedicate this book to my family.
I love you all so very much..

Chapter One

Annie Benson rushed to the park across the street from the restaurant where she worked in Isleton, California. The benches filled up quickly at lunchtime; if she didn't hurry she wouldn't find a place to sit. She slid into the last available seat and struggled to catch her breath.

Tears filled her eyes as she glanced around the beautiful park where she and Alex used to meet and have lunch. He had always told her worrying didn't accomplish anything and she knew it couldn't be good for the babies, but what was the answer? She couldn't continue to work eight hours a day standing on her feet. At seven and a half months pregnant with the twins, her ankles were already swelling. What would it be like in another month? Somehow she had to pay the rent on her tiny trailer and buy food. Alex had died so suddenly they hadn't had a chance to start a savings account.

When she and Alex turned eighteen and had to leave the orphanage, they decided to get married. They weren't in love, but they were best friends. Alex had been in a wheelchair and needed her to take care of him, and she had no family and nowhere to go.

She knew if he were here, he'd tell her to pray about the situation she found herself in, but what kind of a God would allow her to get pregnant and then take her husband? One who obviously didn't care about her, so what good would it do to pray? None. Somehow, she'd have to manage on her own. She glanced at her watch. *Lunch break's over.* She sighed. *Better get back to work.*

That evening, Annie stopped by the post office on her way home. As soon as she unlocked the door to her tiny one room trailer, she went in to change into something more comfortable. At this point in her pregnancy, there wasn't much of anything that made her comfortable.

Annie grabbed a bottle of water from the tiny apartment sized refrigerator, and sat in the gold chair that had come with the gold, and green plaid sofa and scarred oak coffee table when she'd rented the trailer. It wasn't much, but it was all she could afford and it was within walking distance of the restaurant where she worked. She couldn't afford a car, so she had to live close to her job.

As she shuffled through her mail, one item caught her attention. She turned the envelope over and read the name at the top left-hand corner. GATTLER, STALKS and WHITMIRE, ATTORNEYS-AT- LAW. Why would she be getting a letter from an attorney? It must have something to do with Alex.

She slid the folded paper out of the envelope. Her eyes widened as she read the letter. Her great aunt had left her property to Annie? Why would a great aunt she didn't even know she had, leave her a small ranch in Wyoming? Annie's first reactions were a combination of hurt and anger. Obviously since she received the letter, this aunt had known she existed. Why hadn't she contacted her before now, instead of leaving her to be raised in an orphanage thinking she had no family? Because she hadn't wanted her, just like no one else had ever wanted her, except Alex. He was the only one who had ever wanted her and he was gone now.

After thinking about this her feelings started to change, and she began to get excited. A home of her very own and in a brand new place, but how could she get to Wyoming? She slipped her shoes back on and walked to the corner to use the pay phone. After looking up the number, she called the Greyhound Bus Depot to get the rates from the Sacramento NE station to Rexburg, Idaho, the closest station to Yellowstone City,

Wyoming, her new home.

Annie had enough money to buy a bus ticket to get her there and according to the letter; her aunt had left her a small bank account. If she was very careful she could live on it until after the babies were born and she got back on her feet. Then she'd have to find someone reliable to watch the twins and get a job to support them. It would be hard by herself but she'd manage. Nineteen hours on a bus was a long time in her condition, but she could do it. She smiled for the first time since she'd lost Alex. Annie called the Greyhound station back and made a reservation for a seat on the bus the following afternoon.

Next she called her boss and her landlord to let them know she'd be moving. She explained about her inheritance and apologized for the short notice, and they were both very understanding and wished her well. The last call she made was to Miss Caroline at the orphanage. She'd raised Annie. They'd always kept in touch and Annie knew she'd really miss her; Miss Caroline was like a mother to her.

Annie spent the evening packing her few belongings into a duffel bag that would be easier to carry than a suitcase. The next afternoon at three-thirty, her neighbor dropped her off at the bus station in Sacramento on her way to work. At 4:10 pm, she boarded the bus. Nineteen hours and fifty minutes later, she arrived in Rexburg, Idaho. Excitement filled her at the thought of what might lie before her in this brand new place as she lifted her duffel bag and walked to the door of the bus. She only had ten dollars to her name but somehow she'd find a way to get from here to Yellowstone City.

******

Gabriel St. Nick noticed the bus pull up as he finished loading the new saddle into the back of his truck. A young woman with auburn hair stepped up to the doorway catching his attention. From her appearance he'd guess she was about eight months pregnant. The ground was still quite icy from their last snowstorm, it certainly wouldn't do for her to fall. Since she appeared to be alone, he rushed over to assist her.

"Good morning, may I help you down?" Gabe offered her his hand. "The ground is still pretty icy." She smiled and placed her small hand in his much larger one. He balanced her until she stood safely on the pavement; he enjoyed the feel of her soft hand in his. She was lovely, small in stature, with smooth creamy skin, and eyes a brilliant green. The color reminded him of fresh new leaves budding in the spring.

"Thank you, I appreciate your help.

"You're welcome. I'm Dr. Gabriel St. Nick. Do you live in Rexburg, or are you just here for a visit?"

"This is my first time here. I'm Annie Benson; my aunt left me a small ranch in Wyoming and I'm here to claim it. Could you tell me how I might find transportation from here to Yellowstone City?"

Gabe wondered at the pleasure he experienced at her statement. He was attracted to her even in her condition. She didn't mention a husband or boyfriend and he couldn't say he was sorry about that. He'd like to get to know her. Katie walked up and he introduced them. "Annie Benson, this is my sister Katie St. Nick, she and I are about to head back to Yellowstone City right now. I'm the local doctor there and Katie teaches kindergarten. You're welcome to ride with us if you'd like." Gabe noticed her hesitation. "We're perfectly safe, I promise."

"It's nice to meet you, Annie," Katie said. "Come on, Gabe will carry your bag, we can chat on the way back and get acquainted. It'll be nice to have some female companionship for a change, not that I don't enjoy your company too Gabe." She grinned.

******

Annie liked Katie immediately and hoped they could become friends. Her brother seemed gentle and kind as well. He certainly didn't look like any doctor she'd ever seen with his tall muscular frame that didn't sport an ounce of fat, gorgeous blue eyes, and dark brown hair that barely brushed his collar. An instant attraction seemed to flare between them, but surely it was her imagination no one would be attracted to her in her condition. But that was okay she'd make it just fine on her own. She'd promised herself when she lost Alex she wouldn't let anyone that close again, because it hurt too much to lose them and she didn't ever want to go through that kind of pain again.

Katie slid into the middle of the front seat and Annie climbed in by the door of the big Ford crew cab pickup. She admired the soft leather upholstery, the color a shade lighter than the metallic tan on the outside. "Nice truck."

"Thanks, I had it delivered last week," Nick said. "I decided it was time for a new one."

"To my relief! I don't have to ride all this way in his farm truck." Katie grinned.

"And when did you ever ride here in my farm truck?" Gabe glanced at her.

"Well, I didn't, but I just knew there was going to come a time when mom needed hers and I was going to have to ride in that thing for sure." Katie teased. "Actually to be totally honest, he used mom's truck. Once in a great while I get to ride in his corvette, now that's a treat."

"Okay, now if you're being *totally* honest." Gabe raised his eyebrows as he glanced over at her. "How many times have I taken you for a ride in my vette?"

"Several." Katie admitted laughing.

Annie enjoyed their bantering. It put her at ease and helped her relax.

"Where in Yellowstone City are you going, Annie?" Katie changed the subject.

"I'm not sure; my Aunt left me a small ranch. I need to stop by the lawyer's office, Gattler, Stalks, & Whitmore to pick up the keys and sign some papers if it isn't too much trouble."

"That's no problem. It's on our way." Gabe assured her.

"Mr. Gattler sent me this letter." She pulled it from her purse. "It says the property is located at Route 3 Box 500 B. Do you know where that is?"

Gabe glanced at her and then returned his eyes to the road. "You're Molly Cromwell's niece?"

"Molly Cromwell was my aunt's name."

"She and our mother were best friends," Katie said.

Annie had to swallow against the lump that formed in her throat at Katie's words. They knew her aunt.

"Your place is right next to mine." Gabe interrupted her thoughts. "Workers have been out there painting and the roofers just finished putting on new shingles. They laid new carpets and floors a few days ago. It should be ready for you to move in."

"I never even met my aunt." Annie glanced at Gabe and then Katie. "Why would she do all of this for me? My parents died in an accident when I was seven. She let me be raised in an orphanage." It's obvious she knew where I was, why didn't she send for me?" Annie wiped at the tears that managed to escape even though she tried hard to control her emotions in front of these strangers.

"Molly was a warm and loving person, Annie, but she was crippled from childhood by polio so I presume that's why. It was a very slow process for her to even make it up the stairs at night and back down in the morning. A lady came in twice a week to help her and clean house." I'm sure she felt you'd be better off with someone that could take care of you." Gabe explained.

"I just figured it was because she didn't want me."

"I would never believe that." Gabe glanced at her. "Knowing your aunt she would have taken you in, in a minute, if she'd been able to."

"Gabe was your aunt's doctor and he's right, Molly was very sweet." Katie smiled and patted Annie's hand gently.

Gabe parked in front of the lawyer's office. When they went inside Annie walked up to the young woman at the front desk.

"How can I help you?" She asked.

"I'm Annie Benson and I'm here to see Mr. Gattler." Annie handed her the letter she had received in the mail.

The receptionist opened and read the letter. "Please have a seat and I'll be right back."

She disappeared down the hall and in just a few minutes she was back.

"Mrs. Benson, would you follow me please?"

"Did you hear what she said?" Katie asked. "I wonder where her husband is and why she hasn't mentioned having one?"

******

"I don't know, I was just thinking the same thing." Gabe ran a hand through his hair and sat back in the chair crossing an ankle over his opposite knee. "I suppose she'll tell us in due time."

Chapter Two

Annie returned a few minutes later and they left the lawyers office.

"Well, its official now, the ranch belongs to me." She grinned as Gabe pulled out of the parking lot. "I can't wait to see it."

He smiled at the excitement dancing in her pretty green eyes. She was lovely and he had to remind himself, she was also pregnant and married. How could he be so attracted to her, when she was off limits? *Lord, I could use some help here.*

"It won't take long to get there." Gabe smiled. "It's about five miles out of town, but before we go we should stop by the utility companies to make sure you have electricity and a phone. Also you might want to get a few groceries. It looks like snow, so it may be a few days before you can get back into town."

Gabe drove the few blocks and parked. Annie went in the door of the building that housed the electric company on one side and the phone company on the other, very convenient. She was only gone a few minutes. "The electricity is on at the ranch but since this is Friday, I won't have a telephone until Monday."

"Well, I'm relieved to know you'll have power at least," Gabe drove to the grocery store and found a parking place by the door. When Annie came out she only had one small bag with a can of hot chocolate and a gallon of milk. "Annie, there isn't any food at the ranch."

"That's okay I brought a few things with me, I'll be fine."

All she had was a duffel bag there couldn't be much in it to eat. He wondered if she was short on funds, but he didn't feel it was his place to ask so he headed out to the ranch.

Fifteen minutes later they turned off onto a gravel driveway lined with snow covered pine trees. The two-story Victorian style house was painted yellow with dark green shutters. A wide porch with white railing stretched across the front of the house and matching rails along the six steps leading to the front door. Annie's eyes brightened and she gasped; a wide smile crossed her face when she saw her new home for the first time.

"Oh my, I love it! It's perfect." She grinned at Gabe and Katie. "I can't believe it's mine. I've never had anything so grand." She nearly fell out of the truck in her haste to see the inside.

"Whoa, hold on, you don't want to fall and hurt yourself." Gabe came around and helped her down. "Hold the rail and be careful it's still a little icy." He grabbed her duffel bag and Katie carried the grocery sack. Annie unlocked the front door and Gabe had to smile at the awe on her face as they stepped inside. "Where do you want me to put your bag?" He asked.

"You can set it right there." She indicated a wooden high backed chair with a dark green cushion, which sat across the foyer from the stairway that led to the second floor. To the left was a large dining room and kitchen with a laundry room and bath off of it. To the right a living room with a big fireplace that faced the dining room. On each side of it were wood bookcases. The doors and window frames were dark mahogany, matching the bookcases, and furniture in the dining and living room. A gorgeous grandfather clock stood in the entryway.

"It's beautiful. I've never seen such lovely things. Is this actually real?"

Annie looked at Gabe as if she thought someone would burst in at any minute and tell her this was all a dream.

"Yes, Hon, it's all yours and no one can take it away from you." Katie set the milk in the refrigerator and handed the hot chocolate to Annie.

"Let's get you off of your feet, Annie. You need some rest." She sat in a forest green recliner and he flipped the handle to put her feet up.

Once she was settled Gabe brought in some wood. While he started a fire Katie sat down on the floral sofa across from Annie.

"I noticed the receptionist called you Mrs. Benson, Annie. If it isn't too forward of me to ask; where's your husband?"

"Katie!" Gabe couldn't believe she had just asked that.

"No really, it's all right. I know you must wonder," Annie said. "I'm a widow, my husband died from pneumonia six months ago."

"Oh, I'm so sorry," Katie said.

"Yes, I'm very sorry too for your loss, Annie," Gabe said. "If there is anything you need please don't hesitate to let us know."

"Thank you so much for taking me by the lawyer's office and for bringing me home."

"You're welcome. If there's

anything else we can do let us know."

He stacked the wood box full. "That should last you until tomorrow. Get some rest. We'll let ourselves out and lock the door."

Gabe decided he'd come back and check on her later that evening. It looked as if it might snow again anytime. He wasn't real comfortable with leaving her here alone without a phone. He climbed in and started the truck.

"Gabe, it concerns me that Annie didn't buy any groceries? Do you think she's low on money? She couldn't have much in that bag in the way of food."

"I don't know, I wondered the same thing, Katie. It concerns me too, but that's not something you can just come out and ask. I'll mention it to mom when I take you home. "

"Good idea she'll know what to do. Annie's very pretty, nice too." Katie grinned. "I noticed you admiring her."

"She's pregnant, Katie." Gabe backed up and headed down the driveway to the road. "She'll be my patient soon. I'm just concerned about her health."

"Right." Katie looked at him. "She's not married as we thought, so there's nothing wrong with you being attracted to her."

"Katie, I told you she's a patient."

"I know what you told me but I have eyes, Gabe. I can see your interest in her is more than a patient. I've seen you with Rachelle and this is different."

What could he say? She was right and he'd be less than honest if he said that he wasn't attracted to Annie Benson. But he wasn't going to admit that to his twenty-two old sister.

"Mother always says you'll feel different when the right one comes along. Who knows, Gabe that may be the reason the Lord brought Annie here. She may be your chosen mate. Believe me she'd be an improvement over Rachelle."

"Thank you, but I don't need you to be a matchmaker, Katie. We have enough of that with mother and Grandma Larraine. Besides we just met Annie and she's still mourning her husband." Gabe reminded her."

"I'm not matchmaking. I'm just stating the facts the way I see them." She grinned.

Later that evening it began to snow. By the time Gabe arrived at Annie's there was at least four inches on the ground and it was coming down steady. He parked in front of the house and as he climbed the steps, he found Annie sitting in the swing.

"What are you doing out on the porch? It's twenty-eight degrees!" He couldn't believe she was sitting out here in the cold.

"This is my first time to be in the snow. I wanted to be out here so I could see it up close."

"You aren't used to this weather so you don't realize how quickly you could get frostbite. You have to think of your health and the baby's."

"I didn't realize it would be dangerous. I would never do anything to jeopardize my babies."

"Let's get you inside." Gabe softened his voice; he realized at her reaction that out of concern he'd been a little sharp.

Annie started toward the front door clearly upset by his comment, but her feet slipped and she cried out as she started to fall. Gabe barely caught her before she hit the ground. The clean fragrance of her soft hair as it brushed across his cheek, stirred his senses. "Are you all right?"

******

Annie saw the concern in his eyes as he held her until her feet were steady.

"Yes, I'm fine. Thank you." She allowed him to hold onto her until they got into the house and then moved away.

"I'm going to have some hot chocolate, would you like a cup?" She asked hoping to get her mind off of the fall she'd nearly taken on the porch. She had to be more careful, the babies were the most important things in her life. She'd be devastated if anything happened to them. She hoped Gabe liked hot chocolate it was her favorite, with buying it and milk she couldn't afford anything else. She'd brought a jar of peanut butter and a box of crackers with her in her duffel bag; they would keep her from starving until the bank opened on Monday.

Hot chocolate sounds good. Can I

help?"

"The cups are in the first cabinet on the bottom shelf." Annie indicated a cabinet right across from where Gabe stood.

They took their hot chocolate into the living room and sat on the floral sofa in front of the fire. "Annie did I hear you say babies out on the porch, as in more than one?"

"Yes, I'm having twins." Annie rubbed her hand over her protruding stomach lovingly.

"When is your actual due date?"

"December 20th."Annie took a sip of her hot chocolate.

"You're only seven and a half months. I'd guessed about eight, but since you're having twins that would explain why I thought you to be farther along. When was your last appointment?"

"I've only been once when I was three months." Annie waited for his reaction. Disbelief clearly showed on his face.

"You've only been to a doctor once and you're over seven months along with twins? Why Annie?"

She glanced over at the fireplace for a minute watching the flames leap and dance around the logs. "I couldn't afford to go. I felt good and I've been taking my prenatal vitamins faithfully. She looked back at him."

There are clinic's you can go to, Annie."

"Not when you live in a small town and can't afford a car. I worked at a restaurant and lived in a small trailer within walking distance. I had no way to get to a clinic. I didn't have the money to pay for more than one visit to the doctor. My neighbor was a prenatal nurse, when I was five months she listened for the baby's heartbeat and told me I was having twins." Annie set her cup on the end table. "I love my babies, Gabe." The doctor wouldn't see me unless I paid up front when I went in. I barely made enough to pay rent, buy food and get my vitamins; I did the best I could."

"I'm sure you did. It just sickens me that a doctor wouldn't see a pregnant girl because she couldn't afford his office fees. I'm glad I don't live there, I'd never fit in. I couldn't have turned you away; I became a doctor to help people that needed me." Gabe glanced at his watch. "I'd better go, it's getting late and you need to be in bed."

He handed her his card. I wrote my cell phone number on the back and this is Katie's phone in case you need anything. I'll pick you up at noon on Monday. My office is in town at the emergency care, I want to make sure everything is okay with you and the babies." Gabe went into the kitchen and put his cup in the dishwasher before he slipped his coat back on.

"I really appreciate that, but my situation hasn't changed much, even if you take me, I still can't afford to pay for an office visit."

"We'll worry about that later; right now the most important thing is that you and the babies are cared for properly."

"Okay, under one condition. When I get a job you'll let me pay a little at a time until I get it all paid off."

"We'll work something out that will be acceptable to you."

"Then I'll be ready. Please tell Katie thank you for letting me use her cell phone." She walked him to the door.

"Sure and if you need anything call, okay?"

"If I do, I will, but I'm sure I'll be fine." His intense blue eyes scanned her face for a moment.

"Goodnight." He closed and locked the door as he left.

Annie checked the windows to be sure they were locked and thought about Gabe as she went upstairs to look around. She loved her babies; it upset her that he would even think she would neglect doing what was best for them. She would have gone for regular appointments before if she could have.

Chapter Three

Annie was amazed as she reached the second floor; it was just as lovely as the downstairs. There were three bedrooms upstairs besides the master bedroom. They were all decorated beautifully. One in yellow and white gingham, one in pink paisley, the third one which was across from the master bedroom was done in red and white gingham with Raggedy Ann and Andy. It was perfect for a nursery, whether the babies were boys or girls and there were two white cribs with matching crib sets. How had her aunt known Annie was having twins? She stood there for a moment; Alex would have loved this room, she missed him so much. Sadness threatened to engulf her but she forced the memories out of her mind and walked across the hall. She couldn't dwell on Alex or depression would get the better of her and if it did, she wouldn't be able to take care of her babies. They were her first priority, her whole world; they were what kept her going each day.

Annie gasped as she stepped in the door of the master bedroom. A beautiful wedding ring quilt in shades of mauve and forest green on a cream background, draped a gorgeous king size four-poster bed made from dark cherry wood. It stood on a cream carpet; a stool with two steps was fastened to one side allowing access to the high mattress. A matching set of night stands flanked the bed and an armoire, dresser, and chest of drawers were neatly placed around the room. Priscilla curtains in the same quilted pattern covered the large window. Several different shaped pillows in a cream-colored eyelet lay against the shams at the head of the bed. Double doors opened into a master bathroom with a matching decor.

A large Jacuzzi tub sat in the corner. She could just imagine how it would feel to soak in it. But it would have to wait until after the babies were born. If she got in, she chuckled, she'd probably never get back out; a shower would have to do for now.

She couldn't believe this. Everything seemed to be decorated in exactly the colors she would have chosen had she done each room herself. How could her aunt have known what Annie liked? For a moment she was overwhelmed with sadness that she had missed out on knowing her Aunt Molly. She must have loved Annie to leave her all of this. How sad they had both lived their lives basically alone without any family.

She decided to sleep in the pink bedroom until after the babies were born. There was no way she could climb in and out of that big bed.

The next morning Annie had just showered, dressed, and poured a cup of hot chocolate when the door bell rang. She opened it and found Katie on the porch along with four other women.

"Hi, Annie." Katie smiled.

"Please come in, its cold out." She smiled and closed the door once they were inside.

"Annie, this is my mother, and my grandmother, Ruth and Larraine St. Nick. This is Karen Vincent, and Charlene Welch. Ladies, this is Annie Benson." Katie smiled. We brought you some food to welcome you to town and to invite you to church on Sunday."

"It's so nice to meet you. Thank you for the food, it was very thoughtful."Annie led them into in the kitchen, thankful she wouldn't have to eat peanut butter and crackers all weekend after all."

"Oh honey, you're welcome. We're just so glad you're here," Ruth smiled."

I'm glad to be here, Mrs. St. Nick. I understand you and my aunt were good friends."

"Honey, you can call me Ruth, and yes, we were the best of friends. Soon we'll have to sit down and talk; I'll tell you all about her, she was a special lady."

"I'd love that." Annie and Katie served each one hot chocolate, and then took a seat by the fire.

Annie, we're getting ready for the Christmas pageant. It's always a big event at our small country church. Everyone in town will be there. The ladies make refreshments. After the program, we'll gather in the fellowship hall to eat. We want you to be a part of it." Ruth smiled.

Annie didn't know what to say. It was obvious they just assumed she'd be going to church. She was rescued from having to comment when Katie said, "I don't suppose you play the piano Annie?"

"Well, yes, I do. But I haven't played since I

left the orphanage over a year ago. Annie glanced at her then changed the subject. "Would anyone like more hot chocolate?"

She refilled their cups and they went on to discuss the upcoming pageant.

"Our pianist recently got married and moved away." Katie explained. "We don't have anyone that can play for church now, or for the pageant. Annie, won't you consider playing for us?" Katie pleaded.

"Katie, I'm really rusty. Surely you can find someone else that would play better than me."

"There is no one else; you'd be doing us a big favor. The pageant just won't be the same without music. We've been praying the Lord would send us a pianist. I just know you're the answer to our prayers."

Annie doubted that seriously. She'd never been an answer to anyone's prayers. But she had to admit she was excited at the possibility of having access to a piano again. She loved to play.

It looked as if everyone in this small town attended Sunday services. Since this was to be her home she guessed she'd have to start going, she certainly didn't want to offend anyone. Besides they needed her to play the piano and there hadn't been many times in her life that she'd felt needed. It was a good feeling to be able to do something to help someone else.

"Okay, if someone can give me a ride. But if you want me to play for service in the morning, I'll need to be there a little early, so I can run through the music at least once.

"We'll pick you up." Katie gave her a big hug. "You're a life saver Annie."

"We appreciate it, honey. Last week we sang without any music and it just wasn't the same." Ruth gently patted her on the shoulder. Well, I guess we had better head for home.

Thank you, Annie for the wonderful visit and refreshments. The house looks great. Molly loved it here and I'm sure you will too."

"I already love it, it's beautiful." Annie glanced around and then accepted hugs from all the women before they left, promising to see them in the morning.

She went in and put the dishes in the dishwasher and then decided the recliner looked awfully inviting there by the fire. The next thing she knew she was awakened by someone knocking. She glanced at the grandfather clock and went to answer the door; she'd been asleep for three hours.

She opened it and was surprised to find Gabe on the porch. "Would you like to come in out of the cold?"

He stepped inside. "I can't stay long; I just came by to see if you needed anything."

"I'm fine, thanks, but that was nice. Your mother, grandmother, Katie, and two ladies from the church came by this morning. They brought me several dishes of food; I won't have to cook for awhile. I really appreciated that and I enjoyed meeting them."

Mother mentioned they were coming over. I'm glad you had a nice visit. I guess I'd better go, I've still got to feed and it's going to be dark soon."

"You have animals?

"Yes, two horses, two spoiled barn cats, a German Shepherd, twelve hens, and fifty head of cattle."

"Oh my, it must be fun to have all of those animals. I've always wanted a small dog, but I couldn't have a pet at the orphanage."

"When you get settled maybe you can get one."

"I might just do that."

"Katie and I will be here to take you to Sunday school and church in the morning at 8:45 that will give you a little time to go over the music on the piano."

"Thank you, I need the practice."

"I'll see you tomorrow then, goodnight."

Chapter four

Annie was ready the next morning when Gabe knocked and she went to answer the door. She stood there for a moment before she could find her voice. She'd thought him handsome in blue jeans, but he was breath taking in his navy blue suit, white shirt and navy tie. She swallowed and said, "Hi, I'm ready I just need to get my jacket."

"Do you have some gloves? It's cold out there." Gabe held her coat while she slipped it on.

"No, I need to get a pair."

"Is this the warmest coat you have?"

"Yes. It didn't get this cold where I lived in California."

"I have some blankets in the truck. You'll freeze in that light weight thing; you're going to need a heavier one here."

Annie didn't object when he took hold of her arm as they walked out to the truck. There must have been at least a foot of snow on the ground. She appreciated Gabe's support as she waded through the drifts, but she moved away from him as soon as he opened the door.

"Good morning, Katie." Annie climbed in next to her. "My goodness its cold out there, talk about a winter wonderland this is definitely it. It's so beautiful with all of the pine trees covered in snow."

"Yes, it is, I love it here. I wouldn't want to be anywhere else."

Gabe pulled a blanket from the back and draped it across their laps. "That along with the heater should keep you warm."

"Thank you." Annie smiled. "The heat feels good."

"Annie, you mentioned it'd been a long time since you'd played the piano." Katie adjusted the blanket so it covered their feet. "Since you love to play, why didn't you and your husband have one?"

"We couldn't afford one." Annie was thankful Katie let it drop because she wasn't ready to talk about Alex, it hurt too much."

A little while later Annie was thrilled to be sitting in front of a baby grand piano. She'd never even seen one up close, much less had the opportunity to play one. It was gorgeous and she couldn't wait to get started, so she opened the songbook to the first hymn and began to play.

******

Gabe had heard a lot of pianists but Annie was exceptional.

"If she's rusty, I can't imagine what she'll be when she's practiced." Ruth said beside him." Molly would be so proud of her."

"Yes, she would, Mom. It's a shame she didn't have a chance to get to know her."

"Yes, it is. She seems to be such a sweet girl, but I know Molly felt she was doing what was best for her."

Gabe listened to Annie play for a few more minutes, when she was through; he helped her down from the podium.

"Annie, you worried for nothing. I've never heard anyone play more beautifully."

"Thank you. I'm glad it sounded all right, it's been awhile since I played."

Gabe led Annie toward the Sunday school rooms. He'd noticed from the time he'd picked her up this morning she'd been a little distant

Was she still upset over their conversation last night?

Brother Chris was standing just inside the double doors. He greeted them interrupting Gabe's thoughts.

"Good morning. This must be Annie?"

"Annie, this is Brother Christian Grayson, our pastor. Brother Chris, Annie Benson."

"I was enjoying your music. We're so grateful to have you here and to play for us. Welcome to Trinity Fellowship."

"Thank you. It's nice to meet you and to be here, everyone has made me feel so welcome. You have a beautiful piano."Annie smiled and shook the minister's hand.

"One of our members donated the piano to the church, it was her grandmothers. Gabe, I'm sure you can show Annie to class and introduce her around."

"I will, and we'd better head that way." Gabe placed his hand beneath her elbow and guided her to class. They found two seats next to Katie and sat down.

******

The lesson was about a man named Jonah who was swallowed by a whale. He didn't want to do what God asked of him and ignored God's request. Could that really happen today? Annie certainly hoped not and she didn't want to find out. It was a good thing they didn't live close to the ocean.

Annie enjoyed the message but she didn't know anything about the Bible. She was thankful Gabe knew where to find the place the pastor was reading from and shared it with her; otherwise she would have been lost. As they left the Sunday school class an attractive woman approached them.

"Hello, Gabriel." She smiled.

The way she looked at Gabe it was obvious to Annie that she was more than a friend.

"Rachelle, how are you this morning?"

"Very well, thank you. Mother asked me to extend an invitation to you for dinner today."

"Rachelle, this is Annie Benson, She just moved here."

The young woman glanced at Annie's stomach raising her eyebrows and for a moment she didn't think Rachelle was going to acknowledge her.

"It's a pleasure, I'm sure." She dismissed Annie as if she was of no consequence.

"Rachelle, I'm sorry, I can't make it today. Please extend my regrets to your mother and thank her for the invitation."

"That's a shame, call me and maybe we can do something one evening this week." She smiled up at Gabe.

"It was nice to meet you, Rachelle," Annie said as they walked out the door. Rachelle blatantly ignored her and Annie felt her face heat in embarrassment. She knew she wasn't anyone important but Rachelle didn't need to be rude.

"Gabe, I hope you didn't turn down the invitation on account of me. I could have found another way home."

"No, if I could have made it, I would have taken you home and gone back. I have another commitment this afternoon."

"I take it she's a girlfriend. Oh, forget I said that. It isn't any of my business." Annie's cheeks heated again in embarrassment. She couldn't believe she'd blurted that out.

Gabe smiled. "Rachelle and I have dated a few times."

It wasn't the fact that Gabe was involved with Rachelle that bothered Annie, she was glad he had an interest in his life. She didn't want a relationship with him or anyone else. What upset Annie was the way that Rachelle had treated her. She couldn't believe that anyone could be so rude.

"On the way home in Gabe's truck Annie commented, "I can't even imagine how awful it would feel to be swallowed by a whale."

"Gabe chuckled. "I doubt that it was very pleasant."

"That's amazing. I'd never heard that story. I've only been to church twice before today."

"I hope you enjoyed it and you'll come again." Gabe glanced at her.

"I enjoyed the message and Brother Chris didn't yell at us. When I went with Alex the minister yelled and pounded his fist on the pulpit. I only went twice and that was enough, from then on Alex went without me. "

"Annie, the Lord loves you. He doesn't want you to be uncomfortable in His house."

"Why would He love me?" Annie looked at him. "I've never given Him any reason to."

"You don't have to give Him a reason, Annie. He loves you anyway."

Gabe had to be mistaken, God couldn't love her; if He did he wouldn't have let her get pregnant and then taken Alex away from her and the babies, but she wasn't ready to discuss that so she changed the subject as they reached the ranch. "Will it get colder than it is today?"

"I'm afraid so, it'll drop below zero as the sun goes down. Please don't be out on the porch."

"I won't, I'll stay inside. I don't want to take a chance on falling. Thank you for the ride.

"I'll pick you up at noon tomorrow, but if you need anything before then call me."

"Thank you, but I'm sure I'll be fine." Annie went inside, then closed and locked the door.

She hung her coat in the closet and went up to change clothes. On the way back down her feet slipped and she slid down the last two steps. She sat there too shaken to move. After a few minutes she slowly stood. She didn't seem to hurt anywhere but she still felt a little shaky, so she carefully made her way to the rocking chair and sat down.

Should she call Gabe and tell him she'd fallen? No, she seemed to be all right. If she had any problems she'd call, she wouldn't take any chances on jeopardizing her babies. She spent the rest of the afternoon reading by the fire.

The next morning Annie held onto the rail as she went down the stairs. After the scare she'd had the night before, she wasn't taking any chances.

Gabe knocked just as the grandfather clock chimed twelve times. She liked that he was prompt, but she wouldn't have expected anything else. He struck her as the kind of person that would be very efficient in everything he did.

Annie opened the door. "Hi, come on in."

"What happened, are you all right?" Gabe lifted her chin so he could see the bruise on the side of her jaw.

"I'm okay. I slid down the last

couple of steps yesterday evening as I came down stairs and hit the side of my chin on the railing."

"Why didn't you call me?" Concern clearly showed in Gabe's face.

"I would have if I'd had any problems afterwards. Fortunately I didn't hit very hard, I grabbed the rail and broke my fall that's how I hit my chin."

"Annie, you have to be careful on the stairs you could have really hurt yourself. It's good that we're going into the office so I can check you today. They walked down the steps through several inches of snow and out to the truck. She noticed Gabe had on leather gloves as he turned the key in the ignition. Warm gloves and a heavier coat were two things she needed, but they would both have to wait awhile. She'd make do with the coat she had, and put her hands in her pockets to keep them warm. The money her aunt had left her would have to see her through until after the babies were born, and she could get a job. She had to have a few things for them, so she wouldn't be spending any on herself.

Chapter Five

The roads were icy but they made it safely to Gabe's office at the emergency care in town. As they walked inside Gabe introduced Annie to Suzie, his receptionist, and Grace his nurse. Annie filled out the necessary paperwork and Grace took her into one of the examining rooms. She handed Annie a gown and showed her where she could change, once she was settled on the examining table Grace returned. "Okay, honey let's get your blood pressure. The doctor will be in shortly."

Gabe came in with her chart in his hand.

"Annie since I don't have any medical records on you I want to do a blood workup." The nurse handed him a rubber tourniquet. He wrapped it around Annie's arm and tied it just above her elbow.

"Try to relax; I'm not going to hurt you. You'll feel a little stick but that's all."

Annie jumped when the needle pierced her arm, but it was more from fear than anything else. She barely felt the needle.

"Easy now, the worst is over," Gabe said.

Annie was glad she was lying down, the sight of blood always made her faint and it was worse when it was her own. "I-I don't feel very good."

******

Gabe glanced at her. She was pale as a sheet. "Gracie, we need a wet cloth here quickly, please."

"Here honey." Grace placed the wet cool cloth on Annie's forehead and patted her shoulder.

"Better?" Gabe asked as he finished with the vials he'd collected and placed them in a container. He pushed an intercom on the wall and asked Suzie to take them to the lab.

"Yes, thank you. I'm sorry; I've never been very good with the sight of blood."

"There's no need to apologize." Gabe finished the exam and listened to the babies' heartbeats. "I'd like to do an ultrasound, Annie."

"What's an ultrasound?" She raised up." Are the babies okay?"

"Their heartbeats are strong. They seem to be fine it's routine, Annie. I always do an ultrasound on my expectant mothers at twenty weeks. Since you're well past that at thirty-four weeks, I'd like to do one now." Gabe moved the ultrasound equipment over next to her.

"This is the machine we use. See this? The end of this resembles the end of a stethoscope." Gabe held up a hose that was attached to the side. "I'm going to put some of this jellylike substance on the end here, and turn on the machine. When I move it around on your tummy we'll be able to see the babies' on the screen here. He indicated a monitor that resembled a computer.

"I'll be able to see my babies?" She asked.

Gabe smiled at the excitement on her face. "Yes, and if you decide you want to know, I'll be able to tell you what they are."

"Really?"

"Yes, so you think about it and let

me know what you decide."

Gabe smiled again at the expression of amazement that came over her face when the babies appeared on the screen.

"See there's four tiny feet, and there are their hands. See their little hearts beating?" Gabe pointed them out on the screen.

"Oh, my!" Tears filled her eyes and Gabe handed her a tissue.

"It's pretty incredible, isn't it?" He'd done many ultrasounds and yet he was always moved by the awesomeness of God's creation.

"Yes, it is and a little scary. I've never been around babies; I know I have a lot to learn."

"I have no doubt you'll do just fine, Annie. What did you decide? Do you want to know what the babies are, or wait until they're born?" Gabe handed her a towel to wipe the jelly off of her skin while he moved the machine back across the room.

"I want to know." She grinned.

"You're going to have two little girls." He smiled.

"They're girls?" Her green eyes lit up and the wide smile that crossed her pretty face caused Gabe's blood pressure to shoot up a notch or two. The attraction he'd experienced previously increased by two- fold.

"I take it you're happy about that?"

"I'd be happy either way, but two little girls will be so much fun." She glanced up at him alarm visible in her eyes. "They're okay, aren't they? There's nothing wrong, is there?"

"They're just fine, hon. As far as I can see everything looks good. I'll let you know the results of the blood test. You can get dressed and when you're ready, Gracie will show you to my office."

Gabe left Annie with Gracie and

went to see his last patient. He was closing early today, since it was his mother's birthday. He and Katie were fixing dinner for her and he planned to ask Annie to join them.

Gabe walked into his office a few minutes later and found Annie sitting in one of the light blue chairs in front from his oak desk reading a book. "You like to read, huh?"

"I love to read. I keep a book in my purse. You never know when you might want one." She grinned.

"That's true." He sat down and opened her chart. "What do you like to read?"

"Romantic Suspense is my favorite."

Gabe nodded as he filled out all of the information in Annie's folder. "That's what Katie reads also. You two should have a lot in common."

"I like Katie, she's very nice." Annie closed her book and put it in her purse.

"We're having a small birthday party for mother this evening with just a few friends. Katie and I are cooking dinner, we'd like for you to join us if you can."

"I don't want to intrude on your mother's birthday. She just met me and I hardly even got a chance to talk to her."

"Believe me, she's heard all about you." He chuckled. "Katie has talked nonstop about you since we dropped you off at your house. Mother can't wait to spend some time with you. She loved your aunt like a sister. The invitation came from her as well as Katie and I."

"Okay, then I'd love to come."

"Good, I'm through for the day so let's go. Do you need to go home first?"

"No. But could we stop at the bank, and somewhere to get a

birthday card on the way?"

"Sure the drug store carries cards, if that's okay."

"That's fine, thank you." Annie grabbed her purse and they went out to the truck.

After stopping at the bank and then the pharmacy Gabe drove out to his parent's ranch. He went through the gate and headed up the long road.

******

"Oh, my! This is beautiful." Annie had never seen a house quite like it. The outside was made of logs and had dark green shutters. It sat on a knoll and had a large porch with five steps leading up to the front door. A three car garage was attached at one end. Annie noticed that just enough pine trees had been removed for the house and a grass covered front yard. A few still resided there. Annie glanced out across the property and saw a pond in the distance. The setting was so peaceful; it made her feel good just looking at it.

"My mother and dad designed the house and then had it built. My property joins moms and dads on this side and yours on the other side."

"Is your house made of logs, too?"

"Yes, in fact it's real similar to this one." Gabe walked beside Annie up to the door and knocked. It was only a moment until his mother and dad answered. "Come on in." Ruth smiled.

"Mother, you met Annie the other morning."

"Yes. Hello, Annie." Ruth gave Annie a hug.

"Happy birthday, Ruth, it's nice of you to include me." Annie smiled.

Dad, this is Annie Benson, Molly's niece," Gabe said.

"Hello, Annie, it's good to meet you. Make yourself comfortable."

"Thank you, Mr. St. Nick; it's nice

to meet you, too." Annie sat in a large wood rocking chair, its rust and navy plaid cushions matched the sectional across from a huge rock fireplace on the far wall.

"Just call me Nick, Annie. Everyone does." He smiled.

Annie returned his smile. She could see the kitchen from her chair. There was a large center island in the middle.

She had barely gotten comfortable when the doorbell rang and Nick went to answer it. Rachelle and an older couple walked in.

Great! Just what she wanted to do was spend the evening with Rachelle being rude to her.

Chapter Six

"Annie, Gabe said you met Rachelle at church yesterday. These are Rachelle's parents, Charles and Marjorie Hanson."

"Hello, Rachelle and it's nice to meet you, Mr. and Mrs. Hanson."

"Oh honey, it's good to meet you, but please call us Charlie and Marj. We're so grateful to you for playing the piano; Church just wasn't the same without music."

"I'm glad I could help. I love to play."

Rachelle put her hand on Gabe's shoulder and smiled. He returned her smile and reached up to pat her hand. Annie noticed.

"Mother, why don't you sit down while Katie and I fix dinner. It's your birthday. We want you to relax and enjoy the evening, you and Marj can keep Annie company and it will give you a chance to get to know each other better." Once Ruth sat in the chair next to Annie and Marj, Gabe and Katie went to work preparing dinner. Rachelle glanced at Annie and grinned, then turned her attention back to Gabe as she sat on a stool next to him while he fixed the salad.

"Annie turned her attention to Ruth and Marj and tried to ignore the fact that Rachelle continued to fawn over Gabe and it was obvious he enjoyed her attention.

"Annie, it's so good to have you here. It's like having a part of Molly still with us." Ruth patted Annie's hand effectively interrupting her thoughts.

"Gabe and Katie told me about Aunt Molly having polio and how hard it was for her to get around. I wish she had sent for me so I could have known her."

"Believe me, honey, she desperately wanted to. When she received the letter about your parent's accident she was beside herself. It was a very difficult decision for her to leave you in the orphanage. But she felt you'd have a more normal life than you'd have with her."

"I would have helped her, even though I was only seven at the time there were a lot of things I could have done to make her life easier."

"Yes, probably so but she didn't

want that for you. She called and talked to Miss Caroline. She was so kind and caring Molly felt you were in good hands and that she would give you the love you needed as you grew up. You wouldn't be saddled with a crippled aunt to take care of. She wanted better than that for you."

"I guess I can understand her reasoning. Miss Caroline was very good to me and I love her, but it wasn't the same as being part of a real family; someone that was truly related to me. I would have gladly taken care of her if she had only given me the chance."Annie sighed.

"Now that I've met you I can see that and you would have been so good for Molly, but she was thinking of you. She really had your best interest at heart, honey. "

"Is that why she left me the ranch?" Annie shifted to try to get more comfortable.

"Yes, she wanted you to have a place of your own. She has the land rented out; two of our neighbors take care of it and bale the hay. They'll pay you the rent now, if you want to continue with them."

"Yes, I do that's great. The house is decorated exactly the way I would have done it, Ruth. How did she know what I'd like?"

"She kept in close touch with Miss Caroline, who sent Molly pictures of you regularly. When she realized she was dying, she was determined to have the house renovated. The wiring and the plumbing were redone, and everything was redecorated. When it came to decorating the inside, she called Miss Caroline and asked her your favorite colors and what you would like in decorating the babies room."

Annie looked at Ruth. "Now I know why Miss Caroline asked me so many questions during the last few months."

"I'm sorry you never had a chance to get to know her. Molly was a wonderful lady--you would have loved her. I tried to convince her to send for you when she got the results of her tests from Gabe, but she said she wouldn't do that to you. She didn't want you to get to know her just in time to lose her. She refused to put you through that. She loved you, Annie, even though she never saw you in person."

"I'm sorry too, Ruth, and for your loss of a good friend."

Annie suddenly felt an overwhelming sadness. Gabe and Katie soon called them to the table for dinner, which took her mind off of their conversation. Time spent at the table with Gabe's family lifted her spirits. The only damper to the whole evening was Rachelle.

"Annie, when are your babies due?" Rachelle asked.

"The 20th of December."

"Oh, my goodness!" she gasped. "I thought you'd be due sooner, as big as you are."

Annie could feel her cheeks heat in embarrassment, which she was sure had been Rachelle's goal.

"Annie's having twins, Rachelle." Katie said and it was obvious she didn't appreciate Rachelle's comment.

Nick said the blessing and the food started around the table.

"Gabe, have you tried out that new saddle you bought?" Nick asked as he dipped spaghetti onto his plate.

"Yeah, I saddled Sandman and took him out for a ride Saturday, Dad. It's great. It was worth the trip to Rexburg. "

"You got a new saddle?" Rachelle wiped her mouth with her napkin. "I'd love to go riding, Gabe."

"We'd better wait awhile, Rachelle, it's too cold you'll freeze. I just took Sandman out for a short time to try out the saddle."

"All right, but as soon as it's warm enough you'll have to take me out." She glanced over at Annie and smiled."Do you ride, Annie?"

"No, I've never had the chance to learn."

"Well, you'll certainly not have the time now with *two* babies to take care of."

Annie could see right now this was going to be a long evening. Rachelle seemed intent on embarrassing her. Annie wished she'd known Rachelle was coming. After the way she had treated her at church Sunday, she would have declined the invitation and gone home.

"Annie." Katie interrupted her thoughts. "I almost forgot, Karen Shepherd asked me to tell you how much she appreciated you playing for the pageant. The kids did so much better on their singing parts since they had music."

"That was nice of her." Annie smiled grateful to Katie for changing the subject. "I really enjoyed playing for them and hearing the children do their parts."

"You play well, Annie, you're a real asset to the church in more ways than one." Gabe smiled.

"Thank you and you two are good cooks." Annie glanced at Gabe and Katie. "The dinner was delicious."

"I'm glad you enjoyed it." Gabe stood to help Katie clear the dishes from the table. Annie started to stand up to help but Gabe said. "We'll do it, Annie, you're our guest. Sit still and enjoy the time you have to relax."

Annie noticed Rachelle didn't follow Gabe into the kitchen this time, nor did she offer to help with the dishes.

By the time they had cake and Ruth had opened her gifts, it was getting late so Rachelle and her parents said goodnight and left.

Annie had a wonderful time in spite of Rachelle's insulting comments. Gabe and Katie had a very loving family and they made her feel a part of it, which she so appreciated since she'd never had one of her own.

Annie said goodnight to Nick and hugged Ruth and Katie as they left.

Once they were on the road Annie said, "Thank you, Gabe. I had a very nice time tonight."

"You're welcome. I'm glad you enjoyed it. I'm just sorry for the way Rachelle acted. Sometimes I don't know what gets into her."

Annie knew Rachelle was jealous. She didn't realize that Annie wasn't a threat to her. Gabe was Annie's doctor and if it hadn't been obvious before tonight it certainly was now, that hers and the babies well being was his only interest in her. He only invited her tonight as a neighbor, to make her feel welcome.

"Annie." Gabe caught her attention. "Grandma Larraine is cooking Thanksgiving dinner. Why don't you join us for the day?"

"I don't know. It's nice of you to ask but that's a day for families, I don't want to impose."

"You won't be, we want you to come. You can't spend Thanksgiving by yourself." Gabe pulled up in front of her house and walked her to the door.

Annie searched his face for a moment, and then asked. "Will, Rachelle be there?

"No, just family," he assured her.

"Then, I guess it would be okay."

"Good, then it's all settled. We

always have a relaxing day and lots of good food." He grinned.

She groaned. "Food doesn't even sound good right now I'm so full, but I'm sure it will by then."

He chuckled. "Yes, I think so."

"Where were your grandparents tonight?"

"They both have the flu."

"Oh, No, I hope they feel better soon. Would you like to come in?"

******

"I better not, I can see how tired you are, and you need to get some rest. I'll take a rain check for another night." Gabe reached up and slipped her hair behind her ear. She was so lovely it nearly took his breath away. When he cupped her chin and ran his thumb across her soft cheek, he felt her stiffen slightly and pull away. He knew she still mourned her late husband and he should go, but somehow he couldn't bring himself to say goodnight just yet. How could he be so attracted to her? They'd only known each other for a short time and she wasn't a believer, as long as she wasn't a child of God, he could never have a relationship with her. *Lord, I know you must have a plan here, I just pray you'll use me to lead Annie to you. .*

"You have dark circles under your eyes. I'd better go. Sleep well and be careful on the stairs"

"I will."

"Goodnight, call if you need anything."

"Okay, be careful going home."

Gabe waited until he heard the lock click before he headed to his truck.

Chapter Seven

Annie went upstairs to get ready for bed but as tired as she was she couldn't sleep. She was kidding herself when she tried to deny her attraction for Gabe. She had thought for a minute tonight that he was going to kiss her. She should've refused Gabe's invitation for Thanksgiving and just stay away from him except for her appointments, but she couldn't bring herself to do that. She enjoyed his company and because of that she worried she was being disloyal to Alex.

Annie forevermore you're worrying for noting, it was just your imagination, he's in love with Rachelle. Get a grip the attraction is one sided. Just look in a mirror and you'll know that his only interest in you is his concern as your doctor. You're only concern right now has to be getting these babies here and then finding a way to support them.

Gabe came by every evening the next two weeks and brought in fire wood for Annie. She really appreciated his help. She probably could have managed to bring in a few logs at a time, but it would have taken several trips each day in the ice and snow, to have enough to keep a fire going. Independence had its merits, but she knew her limitations and she wouldn't take a chance on putting her babies at risk.

Even though Annie knew Gabe was seeing Rachelle, she enjoyed his company and she was looking forward to him coming by this evening to take her to the store. She planned to get a few things for the babies and the ingredients to make two pumpkin pies for Thanksgiving at his grandmothers. It didn't seem possible it could be just two days away.

Gabe and Katie would also be by tomorrow evening to get her to go to the practice for the Christmas Pageant. The only downfall to that was that Rachelle would be there. But in spite of that Annie was looking forward to it, she loved to play the piano.

Some of her fondest memories of her mother were at the piano while she patiently taught Annie to play.

Fortunately there had been an old upright piano at the orphanage and Miss Caroline had continued to teach Annie over the years she was there. After she and Alex married she hadn't been able to play. They couldn't afford a piano and they were too far away for her to go to the orphanage.

A knock on the door interrupted Annie's thoughts. She went to answer it and found Gabe on her front porch holding a large box in his hands.

"Oh, my, come in. What's in the box?" Annie asked excitedly.

Gabe grinned and sat it on the floor. Annie squealed when the cutest little black ball of fur jumped up on the side of the box and yelped. She reached in to pick it up and the puppy snuggled under her chin and licked her.

******

"Oh Gabe, it's adorable." She giggled and her eyes sparkled with excitement. "Where did you get it?"

Gabe loved the way her face lit up when she was excited about something. "My best friend raises them; she's a toy Scottish terrier. I told him last week I wanted her when she was old enough to wean, she just turned six weeks."

"She's so cute, what are you going to name her?" She held the puppy close and hugged her.

"What are *you* going to name her, she's yours?"

"What?" Her green eyes widened in surprise.

"I got her for you. You said you'd always wanted a puppy, now you have one." He grinned.

"B-But I can't take this puppy. She had to have been very expensive." Her beautiful eyes clouded in worry.

"No, she wasn't. She had to have a hernia repaired. They couldn't sell her for full price. She was the last of the litter and the runt besides, so I got her for a song."

Her face brightened. "But Gabe you shouldn't have bought her for me. Are you sure you don't want to keep her?"

"No, I want you to have her. I have a dog already. What are you going to name her? I don't think she'll be very big."

Gabe was glad he'd made the decision to buy the puppy for her. He had debated on whether it would be the right thing to do but now watching her with the tiny puppy, he had no doubt that it was.

Annie knew she should ask him if he didn't want to give the puppy to Rachelle, but she couldn't bring herself to do it. Maybe it was selfish on her part, but she desperately wanted to keep her.

"I think I'll name her Zoë." She

smiled. "Thank you Gabe. This is the best present I've ever received. I love her already."

"You're welcome. She needed a good home and you needed a puppy, so it's a win, win situation."

"You've been so good to help me every since I arrived in Rexburg on the bus, Gabe. I would have had a hard time managing by myself; I don't know how I'll ever be able to repay you for all you've done."

"You don't owe me anything. That's what friends do, they help each other." Gabe wanted to kiss her but he resisted. Even though he'd only known her for a few weeks he'd fallen in love with her. But they had one major obstacle; she still didn't know the Lord.

He enjoyed watching her with the puppy. "Oh by the way, your blood test came back and everything looked good."

"Oh, that's great; I'm relieved to know that my not going to the doctor regularly didn't cause the babies any problems."

"You're fortunate Annie, I wouldn't recommend that."

"I know and I would have done it differently if I'd had a choice."

"Speaking of the babies, I guess we'd better get Zoë settled in her box so we can go shopping for the things you need. We can get some puppy chow too while we're there."

"Okay." Annie put the tiny puppy back in the box with a soft towel to lie on. "I'm going to put a clock next to her so she won't feel alone. Oh, look, Gabe. She's so cute."

"Yes, she is, she suits you very well." Zoë had curled up contentedly and went to sleep."

They locked the door and went out to his truck. Once Annie was settled, Gabe turned the key in the ignition. "All set?" He glanced at her.

"Yes, I'm all buckled in. Oh, Look, It's snowing." Annie glanced over at him with a smile that lit her pretty face. "Isn't it beautiful? I love to watch it snow."

"Yes, it is." Gabe pulled away from the house and started down the driveway to the road. The truck slid as they hit the pavement and Annie gasped. "Are we going to make it?"

"It's okay I'm used to driving in this weather. We don't want to stay too long though because it'll accumulate on the roads fairly quick with it coming down this heavy."

"I'll hurry; I just want to get a few groceries and some clothes for the babies. I'll feel so much better knowing I have something to put on them when I go into labor."

"You don't have any clothes for the babies?" Gabe asked. He guessed he shouldn't be surprised. She'd said she'd barely made ends meet. She probably didn't have the money to buy clothes.

Her face turned bright red and he realized he'd embarrassed her. He certainly never meant to do that.

"No, I didn't have the money to buy anything extra. My aunt left me some money and I thought I'd use just a little of it to buy a few things. I don't plan to spend very much. I know I'll need it to live on until after the babies are born and I can get a job to support us."

"I'm sorry, Annie I shouldn't have said that. I didn't mean to embarrass you."

"No, No that's okay. I'm sure you'd wonder why I'm not more prepared."

Annie noticed there was only one restaurant in town what if they didn't need any help? Waitressing was all she'd ever done, she didn't know anything else. If she couldn't get on there she didn't know what she'd do."

They arrived at the department store in town and Gabe helped Annie down from the truck. "Be careful it's slick."

They went inside and she bought the things she needed while Gabe grabbed a bag of puppy chow and then they went to check out.

He offered to pay the whole bill but she wouldn't let him. "I'll get the puppy chow. I brought you the puppy and I intend to provide the first bag of food for her and that's not negotiable."

Gabe carried the grocery sack in one hand and held onto Annie with the other, as they went out and got into the truck. It had started snowing hard and the ground was getting slick.

"Are we going to make it home?"

"We should be okay. We'll take it slow."

They had almost made it back to Annie's when they hit a slick spot in the road. But Gabe quickly got it under control.

"I'm sorry, Gabe I shouldn't have asked you to come out in this weather. Your excellent driving was all that kept us from having an accident."

Annie, there are times we have to be out in it; we just have to be extremely careful."

******

Annie slipped twice on the icy steps and would have fallen if it hadn't been for Gabe's quick reflexes. "I'll give you a cup of hot chocolate to warm you up, if you don't think staying will make it unsafe for you to drive home." Annie offered as they reached her front door.

"I'll come in for a little while. I can

drive across the pasture, that way I can kick in my four wheel drive and it'll get me there."

Annie went into the kitchen to check on the puppy. She was still snuggled up fast asleep. Gabe came up behind her.

"She seems perfectly content. Where do you want me to put the puppy chow?"

"Here in the laundry room will be fine for now." Annie opened the door so Gabe could carry the food in and set it down.

"I'll stir up the coals and start a fire so you can warm up," Gabe said.

"Okay, I'll fix the hot chocolate while you do that, how about some popcorn to go with it?"

"Sounds good to me, I like popcorn." He grinned.

Chapter Eight

A Few minutes later Annie came in with two hot chocolates and a big bowl of popcorn on a tray.

"Here let me get that for you." Gabe put the tray on the coffee table and then sat beside Annie on the sofa.

He took the mug of chocolate from Annie and grabbed a hand full of popcorn to go with it. She handed him a napkin and took some for herself. "Oh, that fire feels so good."

"Yes, it does. Annie, would you mind to tell me a little about yourself and your husband? If it's too painful and you don't want to talk about it I'll understand."

"It's okay. What do you want to know?"

"How you met, if you had a happy marriage. I'd just like to know a little about you and your life before you moved here."

"Actually we grew up together. Alex was the first person to befriend me when I arrived at the orphanage." Annie sat the hot chocolate on the table. "I was so scared and he came over and sat next to me. He said his name was Alex and he was seven and a half. He asked my name and told me not to be afraid he'd be my friend." She smiled at the memory. "I had just turned seven and from that day forward we did everything together." Annie watched the fire leap against the logs for a minute as tears welled in her eyes.

"When we were seventeen we signed up to go on a skiing trip. I came down with the flu the evening before we were supposed to leave so I didn't get to go." She swallowed hard before continuing and pulled one of the throw pillows into her lap and wrapped her arms around it.

"That evening, Miss Caroline came into my room and I knew by the expression on her face, something was very wrong." She sighed dejectedly. "She told me that Alex had an accident learning to ski and he was going to be paralyzed from the waist down for the rest of his life." She blinked and a tear rolled down her cheek. Gabe reached up and wiped it away. His touch so gentle her heart nearly skipped a beat.

"I'm sorry, Annie I can't even imagine what you were feeling that night."

"Alex was so active, Gabe. I was devastated for him. I just couldn't believe this could happen to him. I had to go to the hospital, I wanted to be with him when he woke up and they told him the news. Fortunately I was feeling better so Miss Caroline took me to see him. Alex dealt with it better than I thought he would. He told me he had accepted Jesus two weeks before the accident in a revival meeting and he said the Lord had a purpose for all things that happen."

"He was right Annie. Sometimes it's hard for us to understand but the Lord has a plan for all of our lives."

Annie wasn't sure how she felt about that so she didn't comment, she just continued on with her story. "The one thing Alex wanted more than anything else in the world was to get married and have a child. It was his lifelong dream but he was convinced that he would never be able to see it happen. I'd never seen him so sad and depressed. He told me he knew no one would want to marry a cripple who was unable to have children."

Gabe took hold of her hand and she glanced up at him for a moment and then continued. "When we turned eighteen and were about to be released from the orphanage, I had no family and nowhere to go so I told Alex I would marry him and give him a child. I didn't love him as a mate, but I did love him as a friend and I could do this for him. We checked with Alex's doctor since we couldn't get pregnant in the normal way and he suggested artificial insemination. As I'm sure you know it's expensive, so I went to work as a waitress to try to help save the money we needed."

Annie got up from the sofa and walked over to the window. It was still snowing she noticed.

"We finally made it. It was amazing how thorough they were in matching us as close as possible with coloring and background so the child would have as much of Alex's personality traits and coloring as possible. Alex was ecstatic when we found out I was pregnant. I'd never seen him so happy, when I was six weeks along." Tears ran down her face and Annie wiped them away. "Alex contracted pneumonia. The doctors did everything they could but his body just couldn't fight it off and we lost him. He was my best friend, Gabe, and I miss him so much."

"I'm so very sorry, Annie." He came up behind her and placed his hands on her shoulders.

"Alex wanted these babies so

bad, Gabe, and he'll never get to see them. If God is so loving, why would He let me get pregnant and then take Alex before he even had a chance to be the father he so desperately wanted to be? I just don't understand."

Gabe turned her to face him and wiped her tears with his handkerchief. "God didn't do this, Sweetheart. Yes, he allows things to happen that we don't understand, but He has a plan for each of our lives. We don't know what that plan is, or what factors play into His plan. It's hard for us without being able to see the whole picture, to accept some of the things that happen throughout our lives. But I assure you God is with us through every aspect of it."

"Alex used to tell me to pray when I was upset about something. He said life is like a puzzle and God holds the pieces. Every piece has a place and when all the pieces are in His puzzle, He will return again for His children."

"He's absolutely right, Annie. I've never heard it explained quite like that, but it puts it into perspective where you can understand it. "

Annie heard Zoe start to cry so she went into the kitchen to pick her up. When she came back into the living room Gabe grabbed his coat. "I'd better go so you can go to bed, it's getting late. Thank you for the chocolate and popcorn." He reached down, kissed her on the cheek, and ruffled the puppy's fur. "And thank you for sharing this with me. I know it's been hard for you. Will you be all right?"

"Yes, I'm fine."

"I'm glad you're here now, Annie, and if you need anything I'm close by, just call me and I'll be here."

"I will, and thank you for taking me shopping and especially for the puppy, Gabe. I'll take good care of her."

"I have no doubt of that." He smiled. "Before I leave Grandma Larraine said dinner will be at 2 pm on Thursday. I'm glad you're going to join us for the day."

"I'm looking forward to it." She petted the puppy affectionately.

"Good. Try to get some rest and I'll call you in the morning.

"Okay, goodnight."

Gabe waited on the porch until he heard the lock turn then went out and climbed into his truck. He sat there for a moment and thought about what Annie had shared with him. Their marriage wasn't a love match. He knew she missed her friend but it wasn't the same as mourning a mate. He wanted to share his feeling with her; knowing now that they were two friends that had married to accomplish a goal, rather than because they were in love.

"Lord, you know how I feel about Annie. If she is the mate for me, I pray You'll present Yourself to her and she'll accept you into her life."

It was still snowing so he cut across the pasture engaging his 4 wheel drive. As he came to the fence that separated his property from Annie's he stopped to open the gate. By the time he climbed back into the truck, he was covered in snow and soaked to the bone. The weatherman said the wind chill would be down to about four tonight and Gabe was sure it had made it. He drove through closed the gate and made it back to his ranch in record time. Once inside the house he built a fire and took a shower. He had just climbed into bed when the phone rang.

"Hello?"

"Hi Gabe, I haven't seen you in awhile I miss our time together."

"Rachelle, I explained to you the other night at dinner that we were just friends and you needed to look for someone who wanted a more permanent relationship."

"I don't see why we can't still go out as friends at least."

"I don't want to hurt you, Rachelle but I don't think so."

"I suppose all of your time now is spent with Miss Annie Benson."

"I've been helping her yes, she can't do everything right now."

"Well, can you at least pick me up for pageant practice tomorrow night? My SUV is in the shop."

Gabe sighed, the last thing he wanted to do was expose Annie to Rachelle, but he couldn't refuse to give her a ride. "I'll come by for you about a quarter to six."

"Thank you. I'll see you then. Goodnight."

"Goodnight, Rachelle."

Gabe thought about Annie, he looked forward to seeing her again the next day and he wouldn't put up with Rachelle insulting her.

******

The following evening Gabe came to pick Annie up and she was waiting anxiously for him to arrive. She couldn't wait to get to the church. She enjoyed playing, but watching the little children practice their parts for the pageant was the highlight of her day. When he knocked she opened the door with her coat on and stepped out onto the porch.

"I see you're ready. You aren't anxious are you?" He chuckled.

"Yes, I am." She laughed. "I've been waiting all day for this. I really enjoy playing the piano and I just love to watch the little ones faces, they get so excited. They're so cute."

"Yes, I have to admit I enjoy it too. That's why I volunteer to help every year." He grinned.

"Annie, Rachelle is in the truck. She called me for a ride her SUV is in the shop."

Annie smiled up at him when she really wanted to cry. But she knew he had a relationship with Rachelle. She didn't have a right to be upset, but she was. "That's fine Gabe, she needed a ride."

When they got to the truck Rachelle moved to the middle next to Gabe. Annie climbed in next to the window.

"Hello Rachelle, how are you?"

"I'm just fine, Thank you."

Annie rode in silence as Rachelle talked non-stop to Gabe leaving her completely out of the conversation.

When they arrived Annie went up to the piano and played for the children to sing their parts. The reminder that Rachelle was Gabe's girlfriend rather put a damper on Annie's excitement. She didn't enjoy the evening nearly as much as she had anticipated. It took about two hours to go through the program twice. When they were through Gabe turned off the lights and helped Annie and Rachelle out to the truck. He took Rachelle home first and walked her up to the door. She shouldn't have been watching, but when Rachelle wrapped her arms around his neck and they kissed goodnight her heart cracked a little. *Annie, you knew he was with Rachelle, you shouldn't have allowed your feelings to get involved, but you did and now you're hurt.*

Gabe came back to the truck and they headed to Annie's. "Thank you for taking me tonight." She unlocked the door. Do you want to come in?"

"As much as I'd like to, I'd better

head on home it's getting late. But before I go I wanted to tell you I'm sorry about Rachelle."

"I appreciated the ride, Gabe, there's no reason for you to apologize, Rachelle is your girlfriend and I didn't have anything to say anyway so it doesn't matter."

"Okay, we need to get something straight, Rachelle is not my girlfriend. We've dated a few times that's all. I made that clear to her also. She wants a permanent relationship and that's not going to happen between her and I. She's never been more than a friend."

"Well, it sure looked like more than that to me when you walked her to the door."

"She kissed me, Annie and I guarantee you it won't happen again."

Gabe smiled at her and cupped her chin in his palm. "Now, I'd like to see the return of the smile I saw earlier. I'll pick you up about noon tomorrow to go to Grandma Larraine's."

The relief Annie experienced at his words brought back not only her desire to smile, she wanted to do a little dance but thought she'd better not try it under the circumstances. She grinned at the thought. "I'll be ready; I'm looking forward to it."

"That's better. "Gabe kissed her cheek. "I'll see you tomorrow then."

"Okay, goodnight." Annie stepped in and closed the door sliding the lock into place, knowing Gabe wouldn't leave until he heard it click and it was too cold for him to be standing out there. When she heard his truck start and pull away she went to get Zoë. She took her upstairs with her, the tiny puppy loved to sleep at the foot of Annie's bed. Annie felt sorry for Rachelle, but she couldn't help that she was glad they were no longer an item.

Chapter Nine

Bright and early the next morning Annie was up in the kitchen baking pumpkin pies. She was excited about going to Gabe's Grandmother's for Thanksgiving. She had never spent the holiday with an actual family before. Annie slid the pies in the oven and while they baked she went upstairs to get ready. She took a shower and got dressed in a pair of teal cord pants, and a rust and teal maternity top that said Babies are

Beautiful on the front. It had shiny little silver hearts in a circle around the lettering. Miss Caroline had bought it for Annie for her birthday in September.

She had just lifted the pies out of the oven when she heard a knock at the door. Annie glanced up at the clock it must be Gabe, it was time to go. She went to let him in and glanced in the mirror above the mantle on the way, she wanted to look nice and for everything to be perfect today for Gabe's family.

"Hi, come on in. I'm almost ready. These pies are still hot will they be okay in the floor of your truck if I set them on pot holders?"

"Sure they'll be fine, let me carry them out for you." Gabe went into the kitchen and took the pies out to the truck. Annie picked up her purse and waited until he came back in to help her. She didn't dare try to walk across her icy front porch and down the steps by herself. All she needed now was to fall.

******

When Gabe helped her into her coat her soft hair brushed against his cheek. She looked so pretty and smelled so good. He paused and looked down at her, his breath caught in his throat. He wanted to kiss her, but now wasn't the time. He took hold of her arm and helped her out to the truck and made sure her seat belt was fastened before he went around to the driver's side.

They arrived at his grandmother's just as Katie and his parents were walking in the door.

He took Annie inside and kissed his mother and grandmother and hugged his dad and grandfather. They greeted Annie, the ladies gave her a hug, and then introduced her to Jonathan, Gabe's grandfather. By looking at him she could certainly see where Gabe and his dad got their good looks.

"Come on into the living room dinner's about ready," Larraine said. Annie sat in the rocker by the fire and Gabe went out to get the pies. After he took them into the kitchen, he sat in a chair next to Annie.

"This is a lovely house, Larraine. It's so warm and cozy, I love it." Annie smiled.

"Thank you dear. We're happy here. We've lived in this house for fifty-four years, every since Jonathan and I married. There are a lot of memories here."

"Good memories too I might add." Jonathan wrapped his arm around his wife and gave her a hug.

She smiled at him affectionately. "I'd better go finish dinner."

"Can I help you with anything, Larraine?" Annie asked.

"Oh no, dear you stay there off of your feet. We'll take care of everything." Larraine, Ruth, and Katie went into the kitchen to finish the last minute preparations for dinner.

"Did you ever get your old truck running Grandpa?"

"No, Gabriel, I didn't. I worked on that old thing nigh on four hours yesterday and I finally just gave up on it. I guess I'll have to take it in to the shop to Tom on Monday and see if he can get it running."

"I looked at it when I came out to bring the turkey and my guess is that the water pump is shot."

"I think you're probably right, son. I kind of figured that's what it was."

"Dinner's ready, lets gather around the table," Larraine said.

Once they were seated Gabe's grandfather said grace and they started serving the meal.

******

Annie had never seen so much food on one table. At the orphanage there was enough for everyone to have a plate, but nothing extra. She guessed there was enough for seconds and there would still be food left over.

Gabe held the turkey platter while she served her plate and then passed it on down. It smelled so good it made her mouth water. She didn't realize how hungry she was until now. She listened as Gabe teased Katie about her new boyfriend at church.

"He isn't my boyfriend Gabe. We've only gone out once." Katie made a face at him and everyone laughed.

"She enjoyed the different conversations throughout dinner. It was great to see how a real family interacted with one another at the table. This was the best Thanksgiving she had ever celebrated. She was so very thankful that these wonderful people had included her in their family gathering. She would love to be a part of a family like this.

Later that evening as Annie was getting ready for bed she noticed her throat was a little scratchy. It hurt to swallow. She hoped she wasn't coming down with something. She was cold so she took Zoë and climbed under the covers to try to get warm.

It was almost noon the next day before Annie dragged herself out of bed and down the stairs. She felt terrible. Her head hurt, she could hardly swallow and she was freezing. She had just started into the kitchen when someone knocked at the door. She went to answer and it was Gabe.

"Good morning." He smiled.

"Hi, you're welcome to come in, but I hope I don't have something contagious. I don't feel very good."

Gabe stepped in and closed the door. He changed immediately to doctor mode. Concern was clearly written on his handsome face as he reached over and gently laid his hand on her cheek.

"Annie, you're burning up." He set his medical bag on the table.

"Sit down here and let me take a look at you."

Annie sat on the sofa and Gabe stuck a thermometer in her mouth before she could say anything else. She rested her head against the cushions.

He checked the thermometer. "Your temps 103, Annie, where do hurt?"

"My throat, I can hardly swallow and I have a headache."

Gabe helped her to lie down on the sofa. He placed a cushion under her head and covered her with the blanket she had brought from upstairs.

He used a tongue depressor and looked at her throat, then took a q-tip and swabbed it. After listening to her chest and checking her ears he said. "I'd guess you have strep throat, Annie but this will tell us for sure." He placed the q-tip into a container and put it in his bag. I'll take it into my lab and run a culture."

Gabe pulled the blanket up to her chin, tucked it around her, and gave her two Tylenol to take her fever down. "I'll start a fire. It'll be warmer in here in just a few minutes. Then I'm going to take this to the lab, I won't be gone long. Where are your keys so you don't have to get up to let me back in?"

******

"They're in my purse over there on the chair." She indicated the rocker across from the sofa."

Gabe was only gone an hour. He put a rush on the test and then went to the store and the pharmacy. He bought some soup and Sprite, went by to check the test results, and then headed back to Annie's.

She was sleeping when he let himself in so he took the groceries and her prescription into the kitchen and then came back in to check on her. He gently laid his hand on her cheek it still felt warm but cooler than earlier. Her temp had come down some and for that he was grateful. *Father please lie your healing hand upon Annie, and don't let this affect the babies.*

Gabe's cell phone rang and he pulled it out of his pocket.

"Hello, Dr. St. Nick."

Chuck Grayson, the sheriff was on the phone. "Gabe, there's been an accident in town. Shane Jackson was involved. He's been taken to the emergency care."

"I'm on my way, Chuck."

"What happened?" Annie asked. "Is everything all right?"

"I have to go into the emergency care a friend of mine has been involved in an accident." He slipped into his jacket but before he left he went into the kitchen and brought her meds and a glass of water. He helped her to sit up so she could take the capsules.

Annie, the test showed just as I suspected that you have strep throat. You need to stay down and rest. I'll be back as soon as I can. If you need anything call my cell phone."

******

Gabe had only been gone for a little bit when Annie heard a key in the door. She thought he had forgotten something, but it was Katie who walked in.

"Hi, Gabe stopped by and told

me you were sick. I'm to stay out of your face, but to take care of you." She grinned.

"Oh, Katie I would've been okay. You didn't have to come over here."

"Yes, I did you don't need to be up. Gabe said he bought some soup when he went to fill your prescription and he wanted me to fix you a bowl and at 4 pm if he isn't back I'm to give you another dose of the meds."

"That was nice; he must have done that while he was in town."

Katie fixed them both a bowl of soup and stayed with Annie. She read a book while Annie slept, until Gabe got back four hours later.

He knocked and Katie let him in. "How's Shane?"

"He has a broken arm and a mild concussion but otherwise he'll be okay. He was very fortunate it wasn't worse. A man just passing through hit some ice and ran a red light, he hit

Shane broadside."

"I'm so thankful your friend didn't get hurt seriously, Gabe. Did the other man get hurt?" Annie asked.

"Just some cuts and bruises nothing serious, thankfully."

Gabe went into the kitchen and came back with a glass of water and another dose of meds for Annie to take. When she woke up three hours later, Gabe checked her temperature it was down some.

"We'd better go it's getting late." Gabe slipped into his jacket.

"I hope you feel better, Annie," Katie said."

"Don't try to get up we'll let ourselves out. If you need me in the night call."

"I will thank you for everything."

About an hour later Annie decided to get up from the sofa and go to bed. She was feeling a little better. Her fever was down and her headache was gone. Gabe had given her strict orders before he and Katie left, to stay in bed, take her meds, and drink lots of fluids. She went into the kitchen took another dose of her medicine, picked up Zoë, and headed upstairs to bed.

The next morning she had just come downstairs when her phone rang.

"Hello?"

"How are you feeling, Annie?"

"A little better this morning, Gabe, my throat isn't quite as sore and my headache seems to be gone,"

"That's good but you need to rest today and take your meds. Even if you feel better I want you to take all of them. Strep is stubborn and it'll come back if you don't completely get rid of it."

"I'll take every last one I promise." She smiled at his concern.

"I have a patient due in about five minutes, I'd better go. I just wanted to check on you before I got busy. Call if you need anything."

"I will and thank you for taking care of me yesterday."

"You're welcome; now take it easy and rest. I'll talk to you later today."

Annie went into the kitchen after she hung up from Gabe. She made a bowl of oatmeal it would be easy to swallow and took it in by the fire. Zoë sat at her feet and promptly went to sleep.

For the next several days all Annie did was sleep, read, and relax in her rocker by the fire where it was warm.

It took her a week and two days to completely get over the strep throat and before Gabe would agree she was totally well. She had missed church the Sunday after Thanksgiving and pageant practice that same afternoon. Gabe flatly refused to allow her out of the house. Plus she didn't want to take a chance on giving it to any of the children so they practiced without music, but she was looking forward to going tomorrow. Annie was looking through her closet to find something to wear when the phone rang. She went across the room to answer it.

"Hello?"

"How are you doing today, Annie?"

"I'm fine, Gabe, other than being as big as a house."

He chuckled. "Would you like to get out for a little while, since you've been cooped up all week?"

"I'd love to, where are we going?"

"Mom, dad, grandma, grandpa, Katie and I are going on our traditional trip to cut our Christmas trees. I thought you might like to go along and get one for your house."

"Oh, I would love to go. I've never had a real tree, much less had a chance to go cut one," She said excitedly.

"Dress warm and I'll be there to get you in about twenty minutes."

"Okay, I'll be ready."

Chapter Ten

Gabe came in and handed her one of his heavy coats. It swallowed her but he rolled up the sleeves and it was much warmer than hers.

Annie was very excited as they climbed out of the truck at the back of Gabe's grandparent's property to find each one of them a Christmas tree. She'd never seen so many all in one place. They certainly wouldn't miss the few they were going to cut. She drew in a big breath. "Oh, it's beautiful and it smells so good out here."

"Hi, Annie." Ruth hugged her. "It does smell good doesn't it? I'm glad to see you're feeling better."

"Thank you me too. Strep throat is no fun." She made a face and they all laughed.

"Don't get chilled out here now. We don't want you to have a relapse." Grandma Larraine walked up next to them.

"That's why she's wearing one of my coats so she'll be good and warm. I'm not taking any chances that she'll get chilled. That thin little excuse for a coat that she wears isn't nearly warm enough." Gabe frowned.

Annie smiled at him. She appreciated his concern and he was right, her coat wasn't warm enough, but they were expensive and she couldn't afford a better one right now.

They walked through the trees and looked around until they each found the one they wanted, and then the men started up the chain saws. In just a few minutes they were loading the trees. Half the trees went into the back of Gabe's truck and the other half went into the back of his dad's. They unloaded a tree at each house and then Gabe and Annie took her tree to her house.

"I don't have any lights or decorations Gabe. I don't know what I was thinking. "

"We used to bring Molly a tree every year when we went to cut ours," Gabe said. "I'm sure there must be some decorations up in the attic. There's probably a stand too. Come on we'll go look."

Annie climbed the stairs to the attic with Gabe following behind her. He opened the door and reached up to turn on the light.

Annie gasped. "Oh my, there are all kinds of things up here. I wonder what's in all of these boxes."

"I have no idea. Keep sakes I'd guess. Look over there." Gabe pointed to several boxes across the room.

"They're all marked Christmas decorations. " Annie exclaimed and hurried across to open them. "Look, Gabe you were right, there are lots of decorations in here, lights and bulbs." She grinned.

******

Gabe had to chuckle she was so cute. Excitement sparkled in her green eyes as she looked over at him.

"I can't believe all of these; look at all of the wooden ornaments. Each one has a year marked on it." She read the date on each one as she un-wrapped a few of them. I think we should take them downstairs before I unwrap anymore, it will be easier to carry them all together don't you think?"

"Yes, I agree. Here let me get them for you and you can follow me down. Be careful. I don't want to take a chance on you falling."

They took the ornaments out and Gabe helped Annie decorate her tree. He had never seen anyone so excited over a Christmas tree. Of course everyone he knew had a tree every year and most anything else they wanted. Annie was so appreciative of everything she received. She'd never had very much and he figured that made the difference. He was glad he had called her to go with them to cut the tree. He'd never enjoyed tree cutting day as his mother called it, or decorating one as much as he had today. Annie's excitement was contagious.

They sat by the fire with a cup of hot chocolate and enjoyed the lights as they twinkled on the tree.

"Oh, Gabe my first Christmas tree, isn't it beautiful? Thank you so much for making it possible for me to have one, and for helping me find the decorations and trim the tree." Annie kissed his cheek intending it to be a gesture of gratitude he was sure, but Gabe couldn't resist he lifted her chin, covered her soft lips with his and wrapped her in his arms. She kissed him back but then as if she realized what she was doing she stiffened and pulled away from him.

"Annie what's wrong? Have I misread your feelings, or done something to offend you?"

"No, you haven't done anything Gabe." she sighed.

"Talk to me Annie, what's going on?"

"I'm just a little scared, Gabe." Annie glanced up at him. "When I lost Alex I told myself I wouldn't ever let anyone that close to me again, because it hurt so much when I lost him."

"Annie," Gabe gently cupped her chin with his hand. "There are no guarantees in life, Sweetheart. But if you don't allow yourself to get close to people it will be a very bleak future. Isn't it better to love someone and have the time you're allotted together, than to be alone for the rest of your life?"

"I-I don't know, Gabe."

"Annie, I don't believe the Lord wants you to be afraid nor does He want you to raise these babies alone. I believe He has a plan for your life and that's why he brought you here, but you have to come to the point where you're willing to put your fear behind you and trust Him."

Gabe stood up and put his coat on. "It's getting late, I better go. I'm glad you're enjoying the tree, I was happy to help." He grabbed his medical bag from the table. "Get some rest and I'll pick you up tomorrow for church."

After Gabe left Annie couldn't get that kiss or his words out of her mind. She cared so much for him but she was scared. Was he the person that he felt the Lord had for her? She was afraid to hope that was what he meant. But would he have kissed her the way he did if he didn't care for her that way? And if he did care that way for her, could she put her fear behind her and admit that she loved him?

The next morning Annie was tired, she hadn't slept well. But in spite of that she was looking forward to the day ahead. They had Church service that morning and in the evening was the Christmas pageant. It didn't seem possible it was only one week until Christmas. She had found some yarn in one of the boxes from the basement and she was crocheting a pair of slippers for each of Gabe's family members. Along with Gabe's pair she also planned to crochet him a neck scarf. She had noticed he never wore a scarf and hoped it was because he didn't have one, not because he didn't like them.

On the way home from church a couple of hours later, Annie thought about what Brother Chris had said in his sermon. His message had been on the birth of baby Jesus. He said that Jesus had come to this earth to save us from our sins, and that He had lived on this earth and died on an old rugged cross in our place. Jesus loved us and would forgive us, no matter what we had done in our lives. He offered salvation as a free gift, all we had to do was to accept it. Annie had never heard of anyone giving away anything free.

They pulled up in front of her house and Gabe came around to help her to the door.

"Can you come in?" Annie found the key so she could unlock the door.

"I'd love to, but I promised dad I'd help him this afternoon. He has a mare that's about to foul and he wants to move her into the birthing stall. We need to move some things around in the barn and get some straw put down in there before he can move her."

"Oh, how exciting, can I see it when it's born? I've never seen a baby horse."

Gabe chuckled. "Yes, I'll make sure you get to see this one. Take it easy this afternoon and I'll pick you up about five-thirty."

That evening when Gabe came to pick Annie up for the pageant her back had been hurting all afternoon. She couldn't imagine what she'd done to strain it. She didn't say anything to Gabe as he helped her into his truck, she was afraid he'd insist she stay home from the pageant, and the kids were counting on her to play for them.

Annie barely made it up onto the podium and over to the piano. Gabe must have noticed her grimace as she sat down on the bench.

"Annie, are you all right?" He came up next to her.

"Yes, I'm okay. My backs hurting, with all this extra weight I'm carrying around. If I get much bigger I don't know if I'll be able to walk." She frowned.

"Gabe smiled sympathetically. "It shouldn't be too much longer; the babies will be here soon."

Their conversation was interrupted when the children came up onto the stage. Gabe took a seat in the front and Annie began to play the first song. She enjoyed seeing the children in their costumes. Mary, with baby Jesus wrapped in a blanket, which was a baby doll, were seated at the back of the stage inside of the stable, Joseph was next to Mary and an angel stood watching over them. Animals were sitting around just outside the stable and the three wise men arrived with their gifts. They kneeled in front of the manager and the children began to sing.

Annie was very touched by the story and how attentive all of the children were to it. Not one of them made a noise or disrupted the program.

They all went into the fellowship hall for refreshments after the pageant. Annie was sitting between Gabe and Katie. Her back was hurting so she could hardly sit still. No matter how she moved she just couldn't get comfortable.

"Annie, is your back still hurting?" Gabe handed her a cup of punch and sat down beside her.

"Yes, and it doesn't seem to matter what I do it doesn't relieve it any."

"Do you have pain anywhere else?" He asked concern evident in his eyes.

"I didn't have until just a few minutes ago, but it's different now than it was earlier, now it feels like it's coming from my back around into my lower stomach. I can't imagine what I would have done to cause it, Gabe. I've been so careful."

"Earlier? How long has your back been hurting?

"It started early this afternoon."

Does it feel like stomach cramps that come and go, or is it constant?"

"Yes, that's exactly what it feels like and it comes and goes. Like right now it's stopped. My back still hurts but the cramps have stopped."

"Sweetheart, you didn't do anything to cause it, you're in labor. We need to go right now."

"She's in labor?" Katie grabbed their purses and coats. I'll tell mother and dad."

Gabe helped Annie out to the truck and Katie climbed in next to her."

"Mom and dad said if you needed them to call, and they'd all be praying.

"Oh!" Annie doubled over and grabbed her stomach. It was really beginning to hurt.

"Annie take quick little breaths like you were panting, as you breathe, it'll help some."

Annie tried to relax as the contraction subsided, but it wasn't long before another one started.

"Oh!" She doubled over again.

"Already? Katie, how long has it been since the last one?

"Only two minutes, Gabe. We need to get her to emergency care."

"Her contractions are too close, Katie, we can't make it all the way to town. I'll have to deliver her at home it's a lot closer, we don't have any choice." Gabe turned the wheel on the truck as it started to slide.

"Are we going to make it?' Annie looked up at him as her contraction began to subside.

"It'll be all right. Try to relax and rest as much as you can in between contractions." *Please Lord, take us to Annie's and help me as I deliver her and don't let her, or the babies have any complications.*

Chapter Eleven

Two minutes later Annie had another contraction. Katie looked at him and he could see the concern in her blue eyes.

"It'll be okay, we're almost there." Every time Annie whimpered in pain Gabe tensed. He hated to see her hurting and he knew it was going to get a lot worse before it got better. He didn't have access to the meds he usually gave to help with the pain; she'd have to have the twins natural birth. He wasn't thrilled about that. The roads were getting worse, they were slick and dangerous. The wipers were having trouble keeping the snow cleared from the windshield, it was difficult to see.

Gabe jerked the truck to the right, the tires sliding over the ice-coated road. He fought the steering wheel, trying to avoid a collision as a car slid through the stop sign from a side road. Annie and Katie both screamed as the truck went over the edge of the road and slammed into the ditch. They were jerked forward as Gabe and Katie's airbags went off. Annie's seatbelt tightened cutting into her shoulder as her head connected with the rearview mirror. Dazed for a moment Annie didn't realize Gabe was calling her name.

Annie—Annie! Are you all right?

She felt his hand against her cheek. My head hurts." She touched her forehead and noticed blood on her fingers."Katie, are you okay he asked as he examined Annie's forehead and placed a napkin against the small cut.

"I'm okay, but what can I do for Annie? And are you all right?"

"I'm fine."

"Oh, Gabe it hurts! Annie cried as another contraction gripped her.

"I know, Sweetheart, I wish I could make it easier." He held her hand until it was over.

"Katie, hold this against the cut on her forehead while I try to get us out of this ditch." Gabe jumped out of the truck.

"Katie, what are we going to do if Gabe can't get us out?"

"The Lord will take care of us, Annie, he always does."

"Oh, Katie, these really hurt." Annie cried, as she doubled over again with another contraction.

******

Oh, no! I think my water just broke." Annie cried as Gabe climbed into the truck.

"I have some towels here behind the seat." He handed them to Katie, and she helped Annie dry herself off the best she could.

"*Lord, please, we need some help here." Gabe prayed.*

"We're stuck aren't we?" Annie handed Gabe the wet towels.

"Yes, but we'll be all right. I called dad on my cell phone he'll be here soon. I'm going to move you into the back seat, I need to check you. "Gabe got her settled just as another contraction started. "Oh, Gabe, it hurts and I'm so scared" Annie cried.

"I know Sweetheart, I'm sorry. Pant as you breathe and try to relax as much as you can. There's nothing to be afraid of, I'm going to take good care of you and the babies." Gabe pulled on a pair of rubber gloves from his medical bag. I need to check you to see how close you are to delivering."

"Annie, it won't be much longer the babies are crowning." Gabe realized that unless the Lord provided a miracle he was going to have to deliver her in the truck. It would be awkward but he could do it.

"Gabe, what can I do to help?" Katie leaned over the seat and took hold of Annie's hand until the contraction subsided.

Gabe pulled his handkerchief from his pocket and wiped the tears from Annie's cheeks. She hadn't said much, she was suffering in silence. He wished he could give her something to make it easier. "It won't be much longer, it'll be over soon."

"Gabe, I see lights, I pray that's dad coming down the road." Katie said from the front seat.

Gabe jumped out and flagged the truck down. It was his dad and mother.

"I'm sure glad you made it. Annie is about to deliver."

Gabe lifted Annie from the back seat and carried her to his dad's extended cab pickup. They drove the few miles to her house and his dad pulled up as close as he could to Annie's steps.

"How're you doing there, little girl?" Nick asked Annie as Gabe lifted her into his arms and carried her up the steps.

"Gabe says I'm doing okay, Nick. But I'm ready for it to be over with." She groaned as another contraction hit.

Katie retrieved Annie's keys from her purse and opened the door for Gabe.

"I better get back to your mother.

Call if you need us. Annie we'll be praying."

"Katie helped Annie change into a night gown as Gabe went upstairs and brought some blankets and a sheet down. He laid them on the floor by the fire and helped Annie to lie down on the soft pallet. He pulled on another clean pair of gloves and checked her. "Okay, let's get these babies delivered."

Katie held Annie's hand as she pushed and labored to deliver the twins. Gabe thought he felt every pain she did as he prayed and worked to safely deliver the two tiny little girls. He handed each one to Annie after cutting the umbilical cords and wrapping them in one of the receiving blankets she had purchased. He finished taking care of her, bandaged the place on her forehead and then tucked a nice warm blanket around her.

Gabe sat down beside Annie and took hold of her hand. He loved her and both of these little ones. He wanted them all three to be his very own.

"Aren't they beautiful?" Annie smiled up at him and Katie. Love shone brightly on her pretty face for the two tiny babies she held in her arms.

"Yes, they are." Gabe answered, Katie nodding in agreement from where she sat beside him, emotion shimmering in her eyes.

A few minutes later Gabe took the babies handing one to Katie. Exhaustion had claimed Annie and she'd gone to sleep.

"They're beautiful, Gabe." Katie smiled as she admired the babies. "They look just like Annie."

"Yes, they do." He looked at them and felt an overwhelming love and protectiveness toward them. *Lord, please let Annie make a commitment to you. I love her so much. I want to marry her and raise these tiny little girls as my own. I feel that she is the mate you've chosen for me, but I know you don't want me to be unequally yoked to an unbeliever. I trust you to work this out, Lord, so I'll leave it in your hands. Thank you for a safe delivery and for watching over us. In Jesus name I pray, amen.*

"Katie laid the baby she was holding at one end of the cradle Gabe had brought downstairs. I think I'll lay down in the recliner, I'm tired. Is there anything else you need before I do?"

"No, you go ahead. If I need you, I'll wake you. Thank you for your help and support tonight."

"You're welcome. I wouldn't have wanted to be anywhere else. I love Annie. I'm just so glad everything went well and she and the babies are okay."

"I am too, honey. Go lay down and I'll see you in the morning."

Gabe laid the baby he was holding at the other end of the cradle with her sister and went into the kitchen to make some coffee. When he came back into the living room Annie was awake. He sat beside her as she gazed at her little girls.

"They're so tiny, Gabe, are they all right?" Annie looked up at him with trust in her eyes.

"They're just fine as perfect as two babies can be." He smiled. "I've delivered several babies, but I still never fail to be amazed at the miracle of birth."

"They are a miracle." Annie looked at her daughters for just another minute. "Gabe, I've been thinking about what the pastor said this morning and what you said last night. I've decided I want to be saved. Can you pray with me I don't know what to say?"

Gabe smiled elated at her words. "Yes, I can, Sweetheart, just repeat these words after me." He bowed his head. *"Lord, I love you and I come before you to confess all of my sins. I believe you are the son of God and that you died for me, please forgive me, come into my heart and be Lord and Savior of my life, In Jesus name I ask and thank you, amen."*

Annie smiled at him and he could see the excitement in her eyes. "I can't explain the overwhelming happiness I feel, Gabe."

"It's hard to explain, but I certainly know how you feel, Sweetheart." He leaned over and kissed her. "Annie, I love you and I want you to be my wife. Will you marry me? I want to help you raise our two little girls as my very own and I'd love for them to carry my last name if that's okay with you."

"Oh, Gabe, I've been fighting my feelings because I was scared, but I know now you're the reason the Lord brought me here. I love you too and I'd be honored to marry you. I couldn't ask for a better husband or a better father for the girls."

Gabe kissed her again. "How about getting married on Christmas eve? It'll be small just family. Or if you want a big formal wedding we can wait and plan one. I want you to be happy."

"Christmas eve is fine. I'd prefer it to be small, with just your family."

"They'll soon be your family too."

"I like the sound of that. I love all of your family." She smiled.

"They love you too, Annie." Gabe cupped her chin gently and rubbed his thumb over her soft cheek. He glanced over at the babies sleeping peacefully in their cradle. "What are you going to name them?"

"I've decided to name them Morgan Alexis after my mother, and Alex, Molly Katherine, after my aunt and Katie and they'll carry your last name. I think that Alex would agree it will be best for their last names to be the same as yours and mine, and that you'll be an excellent father." She smiled.

"Pretty names, I think Alex would be pleased and I'm honored the girls will carry my last name. I'll try my very best to be a good husband and father.

******

The following week was hectic with the wedding preparations. Annie wasn't able to do too much so Katie, her mother and grandmother did most of the work. Grandma Larraine had insisted on making Annie a wedding dress. She had spent the last week finishing it. Annie had tried it on the evening before and it fit perfectly. It was a beautiful gown, with a lace empire style bodice in ecru and a satin floor length skirt.

Christmas Eve dawned cold but beautiful. Snow covered the ground but the sun was shining. Annie with Katie as her maid of honor were in the back of the church getting dressed. Katie had on a red velvet dress with a white satin sash that tied in a large bow at the back of her waist.

Katie had just finished helping Annie button her gown and fasten her veil in her hair when they heard music start to play. "Who's playing the piano, Katie?"

"I don't know; we don't have anyone that can play but you. I can't imagine who that could be." She handed Annie her bouquet of red roses with white peppermint carnations set on a white Bible, and then picked up her own made of red and white carnations.

******

"Katie, it's time. Shane, Gabe's best friend said from the door. Gabe stood waiting as Shane walked Katie up the aisle and then took his place beside him as his best man. Gabe couldn't wait to see Annie's face when she saw Miss Caroline at the piano. He couldn't let Annie get married without this special person in her life, here to enjoy it with her, so he had sent Miss Caroline a plane ticket to fly here for the wedding.

When the wedding march started Annie appeared at the back of the church on his father's arm. As she walked up the aisle and realized Miss Caroline was at the piano. A brilliant smile appeared on her face and tears filled her eyes. His dad kissed Annie's cheek and then placed her hand in Gabe's before he took a seat next to

Gabe's mother and the twins on the front pew.

Annie whispered thank you as she stepped up onto the podium with him. Her happiness melting his heart, this was undoubtedly the happiest day of his life.

Brother Chris opened the Bible and started their wedding vows. They repeated them, exchanged rings and were pronounced husband and wife. Gabe lifted Annie's veil and kissed her for the first time as his wife.

"I would like to present to you Dr. and Mrs. Gabriel St. Nick." Brother Chris smiled.

Miss Caroline played the wedding march for them to walk back down the aisle together. She met them in the reception hall, and hugged Annie.

"I can't believe you're here it's so good to see you." Annie smiled and looked up at Gabe. Thank you for bringing her here."

"You're welcome, I didn't want your day to go by without her, I know how special you are to each other."

"Oh, Annie, the babies are so cute." Miss Caroline said. "I'm so happy for you."

Annie and Gabe cut their cake and opened gifts. She was so tired they didn't spend too much time at the reception. They had taken Miss Caroline to the airport on their way home so she could be with her family for Christmas and then Gabe had insisted Annie go home and rest.

Christmas morning Gabe, Annie, and the twins all went to Gabe's parent's house to celebrate. The babies were passed around so each one could hold them, while everyone opened gifts. Gabe loved his scarf and slippers to Annie's delight. She had opened snow boots from her new parents, a neck scarf from Katie, her new sister-in-law, a beautiful sweater from her new grandparent's, a new coat and gloves from Gabe, and clothes for the twins from each one. She had just thanked them all when Gabe handed her a card that said, this gift certificate is good for one piano of your choice at Piano's Are Our Business. Love, Gabe.

Annie gasped and her eyes lit with delight as she looked up at him. "Oh, Gabe, you already gave me the coat and gloves. This is too expensive."

"No, it isn't. I want you to have a piano of your own and you needed a heavy coat and gloves. As soon as you're up to it we'll go shopping and you can choose the piano you want."

******

"I don't know what to say." Annie looked

up at him. He was so special what could she have done to deserve him. "Thank you doesn't seem near enough."

"You don't have to say anything; I'll enjoy hearing you play, so see we'll both benefit by this gift." He grinned. "When the girls get old enough you can teach them to play as beautifully as you do."

Annie realized the Lord had given her more than her fondest wish through Gabe, her first Christmas spent with a family of her own, and now a piano to play as well. Gabe was aptly named. In her eyes he was an angel and he had the true giving nature of Old St. Nick.

ABOUT THE AUTHOR

Jeanie Smith Cash lives in the country in Southwest Missouri, in the heart of the Ozarks, with her husband, Andy. They were high school sweethearts and have been blessed with two children, a son-in-law and four grandchildren. She feels very fortunate to have her children, grandchildren, father, sister, and two sister-in-laws living close by. Jeanie and her family are members of New Site Baptist Church, where they attend regularly. When she's not writing, she loves to spend time with her husband and family, spoil her grandchildren, read, and collect dolls, crochet, and travel. Jeanie is a member of American Christian Fiction Writers, She loves to read Christian romance, and believes a salvation message inside of a good story, could possibly touch someone who wouldn't be reached in any other way. Jeanie loves to hear from her readers. You may contact her through her Email: jeaniesmithcash@yahoo.com You may join her Newsletter at: http://groups.yahoo.com/group/JeanieSmithCashsNewsletter Other books by this author are available at www.amazon.com

Made in the USA
Monee, IL
12 October 2022